Once Upon a Different Story

Retold Fairy Tales
You Thought You Knew

Kathleen Fox

Once Upon a Different Story

Fairy Tales You Thought You Knew, Retold By:

The Big Bureaucrat Wolf

The Big Bureaucrat Wolf

The name is Wolf. B. B. Wolf. The other guys in the department kid me—there's some real funny guys there, along with a few guys that think they're real funny, you know what I mean? Anyhow, they say the B. B. stands for Big and Bad, on account of I'm such a hardass in my building inspections. Most of the other guys, they take a little cash on the side every now and then, to overlook stuff. Little stuff, mostly, that don't matter much. But once in a while, something not so little. A couple of those clowns, you wave a C-note or two in front of their eyes and they'll turn flat-out blind. They won't see blocked emergency exits, or fire alarms that don't work, or plumbing that ain't up to code. They say they're just helping folks out.

Not me. I figure I'm helping folks out, all right. But I do it by making sure they follow the building codes so the dumps they live in ain't gonna fall over in a windstorm or burn down around their ears. And if that means acting all fierce and putting on some bluster, that's what I'll do. I never would say this to any of the other guys, but sometimes I wonder, just to myself, how many lives I've saved over the years. No way to know, of course, but it could be dozens. Gives me a lot of satisfaction, you know?

My favorite new construction to inspect is down along the waterfront. It's beavers, mostly, down there. And I kid you not, I've never once wrote any of them up for shoddy construction. Hard workers, those guys, and every dam (dam—get it?) one of them a hell of an engineer besides. They do things right.

Raccoons are almost as good—even better with their hands, but sometimes they get a little sloppy on the details. And some of the birds, too. Badgers and prairie dogs, now, their places are damn hard to get into and inspect proper, but one thing you can count on. They always have two exits, just like the code says.

But you wouldn't believe some of the things I see. The piles of junk some of these jokers throw together and call a house. Hell, some of those places, if you called them dumps it would be a compliment.

And every once in a while, I run into somebody who's just plain weird. Scary weird, once in a while, which don't bother me much. Big and Bad comes in handy then for sure. Mostly, though, the weird ones are just odd.

For instance, those three pigs.

Their places come up on my list all on the same day, the addresses so close together they had to be on the same property. When I got there, I found a parcel of ground just barely inside the city limits, a few acres that had probably been part of somebody's farm once but that had been vacant for years. It had grown up to weeds, with old bedsprings and other junk showing through the thistles where people had used it as a dump for trash they was too lazy to take to the landfill. Some of the weeds had been cut back, and it looked like somebody was making a start on getting rid of the trash, which I took as a good sign.

Then I saw the first house. I kid you not, it was built out of straw. Now, I've seen a few houses where they stack straw bales up, pin them together with rebar, and plaster them over. Cozy little places when they're done right, and cheap, too, if you don't count all the sweat equity.

This wasn't like that. This knucklehead had tied bundles of straw together with twine and stood them up against each other to make walls for a little shack, with a couple of ropes run around the whole thing to more or less hold it together. He had salvaged an old door from somewhere and hung it on a rickety frame at the front, so crooked I didn't see how it could even open. An old window was stuck into the straw on one side, looking like nothing was holding it there but luck. And the crowning touch was the roof—a battered old pickup topper perched on top of the whole mess like a hat that didn't quite fit.

The shack didn't just violate every building code in the book; it violated logic, common sense, and the law of gravity. Hell, I didn't even dare knock on the door for fear the whole flimsy mess would come down.

This was clearly a case for the Big Bad Wolf. Somebody this dumb needed to have some sense scared into him. I put a little growl into my voice. "Building inspection. I need to check out your building."

No answer.

"I gotta check; it's the law. Please open the door."

Still no answer.

I went close enough to look through the window. A scrawny little pig was standing in the middle of the floor like he was hoping if he stayed real still I wouldn't notice him. Fat chance—hell, there were so many gaps in the straw, I could hear the little hambone breathing. Besides, I saw another clear violation that was—if you don't mind my saying so—the last straw. The idiot figured to do his cooking and heat the place with a charcoal grill.

I took the growl up a couple of notches. "I know you're in there. Let me in!"

This finally got a response, in a squeaky little voice that sounded scared half to death. "Go away! This is my house!"

"I know it's your house. The law says it has to be inspected."

"That's unconstitutional. I have the right in my own house to be secure from unreasonable search and seizure."

Oh, geez. Another don't-regulate-me nut. If they didn't want to be bothered by petty little details like building codes, why didn't they keep their lunatic-fringe lifestyle out in the woods someplace?

There was probably no use arguing with him, but I had to try. "And your neighbors have the right to be secure in their houses against the chance—which I have to say is looking pretty high—that your scarecrow hut here is going to blow over in the first strong wind and your illegal heat source is going to burn down the whole neighborhood."

"That's a lie! The specs are designed to withstand winds of up to 80 miles per hour."

"Specs? You mean you had plans for this shack?"

"Of course." He sounded smug now. "We found them on an Internet site about living off the grid."

"And you took these plans to City Hall when you got your building permit?" I already knew the answer to this one, but I still had to ask.

"I don't need a permit from City Hall to build my own house on my own property. It's my—"

Rolling my eyes, I chimed in and said it with him: "—Constitutional right."

By now I was getting sore. The growl in my voice wasn't just for show. "Let me tell you about your rights, buddy. If you don't let me in, I'll report this as unfit for habitation. The city will send somebody with a bulldozer to flatten it, and they'll charge you a pretty penny for doing the work. That's if a good wind don't blow it down first. Hell, it wouldn't even take a wind—I bet if I just leaned on it, I could make your little straw stack fall over myself."

There was a long pause. Then the makeshift door creaked open, and he came marching out, snout in the air. "All right, then," he told me, trying for a macho tone in his high-pitched voice, "You just go ahead and try!"

I have to say, I'm not proud of what I did then. Oh, I didn't get into any trouble at work over it. The guys thought it was funny, of course. A couple of them still call me B. B. B. for Big Bad Bulldozer. And the boss told me in private that, while he couldn't officially approve of my actions, he appreciated my saving the city the trouble of tearing the place down.

Still, what I did wasn't right. Somebody in my position hadn't ought to let his temper get the better of him. It's not professional. But I was pissed off enough to take the pig's challenge.

I took a deep breath and blew it out hard, then another and another. Huffing and puffing, I thought of it—something supposed to make you feel stronger. I learned it from a martial arts video. Then I leaned into that flimsy straw wall and pushed. The straw rustled and shifted under my weight, and the door frame cracked, and then the whole haphazard mess went over. It collapsed into a pile of straw—I saw mice scurrying off in all directions—with the pickup topper balanced crookedly on the top.

For a long minute there was an awful silence except for the rustling of the straw as it settled. Then the pig found his voice. I tell you, I've been threatened and yelled at—it pretty much comes with the job—but this was the most thorough cussing out I've ever had in my life. At first he was so mad he just squalled, and then he started using language he should have been too young to know.

I just stood there and took it. I was feeling half ashamed of myself for losing my temper, so I figured I deserved it. At the same time, I have to admit, there was a little voice in my head saying,

"Damn! I just pushed over a house!" with a sneaking sense of deep-down satisfaction.

By now the pig had calmed down enough to make coherent threats. "Look what you did! You bully! I'll report you to the mayor! I'll sue the city! I'll call the cops!"

"Look at it this way," I said finally. "I did you a favor. Look at all the money you saved. The city would have billed you a pretty penny for razing this rathole."

Well, that set him off again. But he was running out of steam, so it wasn't long till he trailed off into muttering and grunting. Then he said something that sounded like, "warn my brother," and went trotting off through the weeds. I saw he was following a little trail, so I went after him.

The trail led to something that looked like a kids' play fort. It was an uneven square, made with a bunch of sticks stuck into the ground side by side and tied together with twine. The roof was four pieces of blue plastic; after a minute I recognized the sides of what had been a portable toilet.

The pig trotted up to a door that looked like it had come off of his pickup topper. It opened real quick, like somebody inside had been watching for him, and he slipped inside.

"Oh, hell," I said. "Here we go again."

This time I tried a different tactic. As I got close to the door, I could hear excited, shrill pig voices inside. I figured Straw Pig was telling Stick Pig what had happened. Instead of knocking, I stood outside and waited. My theory was that if Straw told Sticks the whole story, maybe Sticks would have enough sense to let me in. I didn't have much hope it would work out that way, but I figured it was worth a try.

Surprise, surprise—it worked. After a bit the voices died down, and I could hear the pigs moving around inside the shack. Then the door opened a crack, and something white came poking through. It was a handkerchief, tied to a stick; after a bit I figured out it was supposed to be a flag of truce. It was followed, slowly, by a pig snout. Sticks himself, I guessed.

"Mr. Wolf," he said, very polite. "If we come out to talk to you, do I have your word you won't do anything drastic?"

It took me a minute to swallow my grin, but I'm pretty proud of the fact that I managed to keep my voice serious. "Mr. Pig," I said back, nice as could be, "I give you my word. My job is to inspect your house to see if it complies with city codes. I'm not here to harass you or arrest you."

Then I added, "Though I do have to tell you, based on what I see so far, it's almost certain I'll have to report your place as unfit for habitation."

The snout disappeared, and the flag of truce was pulled back inside. Then I heard a big sigh. The door opened slowly, and both of the pigs came out.

Straw Pig gave me a wild-eyed stare and scooted well off to one side, but Stick Pig came right up to me. I had to give him credit—he looked so defeated he didn't hardly have any curl left to his tail, but he had a sort of grim determination, too, like he meant to face the worst and get it over with.

"Please go ahead and look inside, Mr. Wolf," he said, so I did. It only took one glance to see the place was pretty much what I expected—a packed dirt floor, a salvaged window nailed crookedly to the sticks on one wall, and another charcoal grill for heat and cooking.

"Sorry, Mr. Pig," I told him. "It has to go."

He nodded. "Then will you do me a favor? Please?"

This surprised me. Offers of bribes usually came from landlords or sleazy business owners. Besides, anybody living in a makeshift shack like this sure couldn't have much to offer in the way of illegal inducements. "What kind of favor?" I asked, scowling to let him know I wasn't the kind of guy who did favors.

"Will you give me a few minutes to get my things out, and then push my house down the way you did my brother's?"

I didn't know what to say to that. He must have seen my confusion, because he hurried to explain. "My brother said the city would charge me for tearing it down. I don't have any money." He waved a trotter at the ramshackle mess behind him. "If I did, do you think I'd have built this?"

This was another surprise. "What about living off the grid and recycling and all that?"

He shrugged. "That's mostly my brother's idea. Me, I just need a cheap place to live. As soon as I get a better job, I'm saving up to rent a little apartment somewhere. With plumbing."

Well, after that, what could I do? I said, "Okay—but it's still your job to clean up the site."

"Deal," he said. He trotted in and out a few times, bringing out a little pile of stuff, and then stepped back and nodded to me, real serious.

I started huffing and puffing. When I felt ready, I leaned against one spindly wall and pushed.

It was pretty much a repeat of the straw house. The whole thing started to sway, and creak, and then it toppled over with a soft "whump!" and a puff of dust, with the portable toilet draped over the top.

It's embarrassing to admit this, but knowing I had the owner's permission took most of the fun out of the whole operation. Still, I had to wipe a grin off my face before I turned to face the pig.

He looked—relieved, I guess, is the word, but still not happy. "Thank you, Mr. Wolf," he said. "But my brother is going to have a fit."

"Your brother? He looks okay to me." I nodded at Straw Pig, who had watched all this from across the yard, the way you might stare while your neighbor's house burned down.

"Not him. My older brother."

Oh, yeah. I had forgotten about the third address on my list. I picked up my clipboard with a sigh. Might as well get it over with. Though truth be told, I wasn't feeling up to pushing over another makeshift shack.

"It's right over here," Sticks told me. "I'll show you."

I followed him, with Straw trailing along behind me. The path took us along an overgrown lilac hedge, and when we came around the end of it, what I saw stopped me in my tracks.

No straw. No sticks. No makeshift junk salvaged from the dump. Sitting in the middle of a tidy patch of mowed grass was a neat little house, foursquare and solid, build out of bricks. It was such a contrast to the last two disasters, I had to check the address on my clipboard to make sure I was at the right place.

As we came up the walk—neat gravel edged with bricks that matched the house—the door opened, and out stepped the third pig. Where the other two had seemed stressed and scrawny, he looked plump and prosperous. Proud of himself, too. "Mr. Wolf," he said, in the tone a supervisor might use to a guy applying for job cleaning toilets, "I've been expecting you. Come in and let me show you around."

The place looked like something out of some magazine on "green living." He had salvaged the bricks, doors, and windows from an office building that was being torn down. He had solar panels on the roof, a composting toilet, a system to recycle gray water, and a wood stove—properly installed—for heat. The place was a tad claustrophobic for somebody my size, but it was well-built and cozy. And everything done according to code; I didn't find a violation anywhere.

"This is amazing, Mr. Pig," I told him as we stepped back outside. "How did you do it?"

"With slave labor and theft, that's how!" Something hurtled past me and hit Brick Pig like, well, a ton of bricks. It was Stick Pig. Straw Pig was right behind him. Squealing and shrieking, the two of them piled into their brother and knocked him flat on his hams. The three of them rolled around on the nice green lawn in a squealing, kicking, punching tangle of brotherly love.

I let them enjoy themselves for a few minutes, but then I figured I'd better stop things before they hurt each other. I waded in with a couple of growls and grabbed a couple of ears, and they settled down pretty quick. I hauled them off of each other and parked them in neutral corners. They were all still squalling, and Bricks was shouting something about assault.

"Shut up, all of you!" I roared, and they did. "All right, now," I said, "tell me what's going on." I pointed at Straw Pig, whose cheek was darkening with a bruise but who wasn't bleeding. "You first."

"He stole our share of the money! It was all Mama had. She meant it for all of us, but he took it all!" The last words were lost in a rush of tears and squalling.

Stick Pig, considerably calmer, chimed in. "He's talking about our inheritance. There wasn't a lot, but Mama said each of us was supposed to get a third. Pearson is the oldest, and he said he'd take care of everything."

"He took everything—that's what he did!" Straw Pig charged at Brick Pig, aka Pearson, again. I managed to grab him before he connected, and this time I held onto him.

"Shut up, Pippen; I'm trying to explain," said Sticks. "Pearson bought the land really cheap, and he said we'd use the rest of the money and all work together to build each of us a house. We did his first. Pippen and I hauled all the bricks, and we built the walls, and we—"

"We worked our tails off!" Pippen—I still thought of him as Straw—squealed. "And when his house was done, and it was time to build Percy's and mine, Pearson wouldn't help!"

"That's right." By now Sticks/Percy was hopping up and down and shouting, so I grabbed him, too. "He said the money was all gone, and after we earned enough to buy our own materials, he would tell us what to do to build our houses—'the same way I built mine,' he said—like he did it himself, when we did all the hard work."

All this time, while I was listening to Straw and Sticks, I'd kept my eye on Pearson. At first, behind the white hanky he was holding to his snout to stop a nosebleed, the look on his fat face was pissed-off in a kind of superior way. He looked like the long-suffering big brother, trying to do his best to take care of the younger ones and not getting any credit.

Hah. I grew up with older brothers; I know better. And by the time the others got to the end of their story, I saw something else on his face. Guilt. They were telling the truth, all right, and he knew it.

"We should sue him!" Straw was back in full squall. "Except we can't afford to pay a lawyer because Pearson spent all our money!" When I tightened my grip on his arm just a tad, he winced and settled down to muttering under his breath. I caught something about "what Mama would think."

Well, I was sore enough by then to feel like giving smug little Bricks/Pearson a walloping on my own account. Get a grip, buddy, I said to myself. I took a few slow, even breaths to get calm and centered. My yoga instructor says breathing is the keystone of mindful action; maybe I should have remembered that before I pushed over the straw house.

After what I'd done to both the straw and stick houses, I was in this up to my eyeballs. It was a little late to be concerned about minding my own business. Oh, I still could have backed off and just done my job. Which, strictly speaking, was to inspect the buildings for code violations, fill in my forms, and go back to City Hall. But, hell, this just wasn't right. I know I'm just a low-level bureaucrat, and most of the folks I deal with see my job as a necessary nuisance and me as a pain in the butt. But like I said before, I see what I do as helping people live better and stay safe.

So I took another deep breath and raised my voice. "Okay, all of you—listen up!"

There was dead silence. I gave them my best business-like tone. "Let's look at the options, here, shall we?" I let go of Pippen and Percy and picked up my clipboard.

"Option one: you two can sue your brother. If that's what you want, I'd be glad to give you my sister-in-law's phone number. She's a lawyer, and damn good at it. Of course, that will cost money, which is a bit of a problem since you don't have any."

I took a step toward Pearson. "So here's option two. It just so happens that I haven't filled out the forms yet for your house. I'm thinking maybe I need to take a second look. The venting on your stove probably needs to be checked out by a specialist. The gray-water system better have an inspection, too. And how do I know those salvaged bricks are approved for residential use? As old as they are, they could have all kinds of harmful chemicals in them. They really ought to be tested. Of course, you'd have to pay for all those extra inspections. But when it comes to your health and safety, money is no object, right?"

By now he was starting to sputter through his hanky, so I raised my voice a little and let the growl through. "Or maybe there's another way to do this. I could hang onto these forms for a while. Say, maybe, until you've helped your brothers build nice, solid little houses just like yours. It would make more sense to wait till they're all done and inspect all three at once, don't you think?" I stepped closer. Being as how he was so much shorter than me, I suppose it might have accidentally seemed like I was looming over him even though I was careful to keep my body language polite. I even smiled at him with all of my teeth.

He backed up in a hurry. "All right! I'll help them. I'll do whatever you say. But I didn't steal any money—it just ran out faster than I thought it would."

"It always does, Mr. Pig." I told him. "Which is why you better figure out a way to earn some more so you can make things right with your brothers. The sooner you get their houses built, the less time the three of you will have to share this one."

Pearson started to open his mouth, then thought better of it and settled for giving me a surly look. I took the forms off the front of my clipboard and stowed them away inside it, making sure he saw what I was doing.

"Just one more thing. Once you're done, you guys will be experts on building green homes with recycled materials. Lots of interest in that stuff, you know. I bet you could teach some classes. I could hook you up with the right people at City Hall."

With that, Pearson perked right up. "I'd like that a lot, Mr. Wolf," he said.

"And, of course, a key selling point would be your hands-on experience, personally building three houses that all passed inspection. Right?" I gave him a hard look.

"Right." He went back to looking surly. His brothers, though, were looking hopeful.

"It's been nice doing business with you," I told them, and left them to it.

But once I got out of sight behind the lilac hedge, I stopped to listen. It didn't take long for the fussing to start. From the sound of things, Pearson was trying to get out of the deal, Pippen was squalling threats, and Percy was trying to smooth things over.

I slipped back and poked my nose around the end of the hedge. "Just one thing I forgot to mention."

It was comical to see the way they jumped when they heard my voice. "I'll be stopping by every week just to see how things are coming along. I bet we'll get to know each other real well."

I waited a minute to let that soak in. Then I gave them all a big toothy grin and headed for my truck.

The
Murdered
Giant's Wife

The Murdered Giant's Wife

This issue of *Downland Today* features an exclusive interview. Uplander Melinda Pettit, the widow of Hugh "Shorty" Pettit, takes you behind the headlines in the "Jack the Giant Killer" case. In her own unedited words, she reveals the lives destroyed by the tragedy of bean addiction.

Now that the trial is over, it's a relief to be able to say some things I wasn't allowed to talk about before. First of all, that whole business about the rhyme. How could anybody believe that something as silly as, "Fee, fi, fo fum, I smell the blood of an Englishman" could be anything but a joke? All those reporters trying to make out that Shorty was some sort of monster, just because of that silly rhyme, that isn't fair and it isn't right. I've tried to tell them, but they don't listen. They want scary headlines; they don't care about the truth.

The truth is that Shorty made up that rhyme years ago, when our son was just a little mite. I remember Tom, when he was barely even four feet tall, hiding behind the bedroom curtains in his footie pajamas, giggling and giggling while his daddy pretended to look for him, chanting that rhyme the whole time. Then he would "find" Tom, and grab him up and growl and pretend to eat him up, and they would both laugh, and then he would sing Tom a lullaby and carry him off to bed. And it got to be a family joke even after Tom was older, and lots of times Shorty would come into the house and say it to me before he grabbed me and gave me a big kiss and a hug. And to think he'll never get to do that with our grandchildren. Oh, dear me.

Well, of course it all started because of the beans. Magic beans, you Downlanders call them, but of course there's nothing magic about them, really. Even though everybody eats them up here, not many people grow them at home like Shorty did because they're such a nuisance. They grow so fast they can take over a garden in no time, so you have to cut them back every day and watch so they don't spread. And you have to be so careful to follow the rules. You can't dump them on compost piles, and you have to report them to Bean Control if you find any growing in the road ditch, and you can't haul them anywhere except in approved containers because you don't dare drop them anywhere they might fall through to the Downlands.

They're good, sensible rules, too. What happened with Jack just proves it. Even after what he did to my Shorty, I can find it in my heart to feel sorry for him, because it was the beans that made him do it.

Something you Downlanders need to understand is how serious we Uplanders are about bean protection. Children get bean management classes from the time they start first grade. They learn the slogans even earlier. Our Tom could recite them before he was three: Never Play With Beans, Eat Your Beans to Build Your Bones, Be a Careful Bean Counter, Only You Can Control Your Beans. We all know how important the beans are to our diets, and we all know how dangerous they are to you. We all see the videos about Downlander addicts and how crazy and unpredictable they can get.

So when Shorty was out for his walk one day and found those five beans, he did the responsible thing like any careful bean manager. He picked them up to bring home and put away. But he didn't have a container, so he put them in his pocket, and when he got home, the beans were gone.

And it was all my fault. It was, truly, because I knew those pants had a hole in the pocket. He told me a few days earlier. So I told him to put the pants by my sewing basket and I'd mend them, but he forgot, and I forgot, and then he wore them again, and that was the day he picked up the beans.

Well, of course we were both in a panic. You see, he was walking in the woods—it was his favorite place, out there in the trees, and he went for long walks there almost every day. So of course he didn't know exactly where he had been.

We went right back out, and we walked those woods and searched, and looked again the next day, and every day for more than a week. But we never found those beans. There was one spot, where a tree had fallen over and there was a hole, but we didn't find any sign of a crack where the beans could have fallen through.

Finally I told Shorty, "Babycakes, you've done everything you can. Either those beans fell through to the Downlands or they didn't, and either way, what happened has happened. You need to let it go."

Well, he tried. He still wasn't sleeping well—he couldn't relax, even when the harp sang to him. But after a couple of weeks he seemed to be getting better.

Then one day, when he was at the Little Giants Club For Boys—he volunteered there, you see, and I got the nicest card from them, signed by all the boys, saying how much they're going to miss him. But anyway, he was gone for the day, and about the middle of the morning there was a knock at the door, and when I opened it there was Jack. Of course I didn't know his name then. But when I saw a Downlander boy on my front step, I knew right away those beans must have fallen through.

"I'm lost and hungry, ma'am," he said to me, just as polite and humble as could be. "Could you possibly spare me a bit of bread?"

Well, he looked like he hadn't had a decent meal in weeks. He was skinny, and his pants were worn almost through at the knees, and his shirt was way too small so his scrawny little arms stuck out of the sleeves. I don't know much about Downlanders, but no matter who he was it wouldn't have been right to leave him half starved that way. I felt sorry for the poor little mite. I helped him climb up on a chair at the kitchen table, and I fixed him a nice big breakfast. While he ate, I asked him some questions, casual-like, and got the story out of him about how he and his widowed mum were so poor, and he traded their cow for five beans—he called them magic beans, of course—and a huge stalk grew up overnight and he climbed it.

As far as I could tell, he didn't seem to know anything about what the beans do to Downlanders. I figured if I could get him to go back down the beanstalk and cut it down right away, everything would be all right.

So I talked to him, real serious, just like his own mother would have done, I'm sure. "You can't come back up here," I said, just as plain as that. "It's against the law, and it's dangerous. I'll give you some food to take with you, and a gold coin to help you and your mum buy some food, and you promise me you'll climb right back down that beanstalk and chop it off at the bottom so nobody can climb it again."

I tried to get him to tell me where the beanstalk was, so Shorty and I could get the hole covered over, but he just said it was somewhere in the woods and he wasn't even sure he could find it again. But he didn't understand why cutting down the beanstalk was so important, and he kept asking questions, and I tried to answer them without giving away too much about the beans. And I was still trying to get him to promise when I heard Shorty coming up the front walk.

Then I had what seemed like a real bright idea. It wasn't, as it turned out, but of course I didn't know that at the time. I figured if I scared him enough, he wouldn't come back.

"Oh, no!" I cried, pretending to be all in a panic. "It's my husband! There's nothing he likes better for lunch than a Downlander boy sandwich with pickles and onions. Quick, we can't let him find you!"

Well, my plan was to hustle him out the back door and send him back to his beanstalk, but he was too quick for me. The crafty little bugger hopped into the oven to hide. Shorty came in just as Jack shut the oven door, so I was stuck and had to make the best of it.

As it happened, what Shorty did then fell right in with my plan. He burst through the door, chanting, "Fee, fi, fo fum, I smell the blood of an Englishman!" and he grabbed me and gave me a big kiss. He was more cheerful than he'd been since the beans disappeared, and I was so pleased about it I just couldn't bear to tell him about Jack. I know it was wrong—goodness knows I've spent enough time since wishing I'd done different—but there you are; what's done is done.

"Why are you home so early?" I asked.

"To count our money, my sweet little wife," he said. "If we have enough, I want to help pay for the new playground we're building at the Little Giants Club."

I fetched the money bag out of its hiding place behind the rutabagas in the pantry, and he sat down at the table and counted. There was more gold that it's wise to keep in the house, as I'd tried to tell him more than once, but he always said he liked to know where it was.

He separated out one stack of coins for the club and put the rest back into the bag. I went upstairs to get a different bag to put the donation in. What with rummaging in this drawer and that to find something the right size, I was gone longer than I intended.

When I came back, there was Shorty, sound asleep with his head down on the table. And no wonder; the poor man hadn't slept well in weeks.

I figured this was my chance to get rid of Jack. But when I opened the oven door, he was gone. Sneaked out and ran, I thought. Just as well.

Then I noticed there was no money on the table.

I hoped Shorty had put it away before he fell asleep, but there was no bag behind the rutabagas. Jack had stolen it—that ungrateful little sneak.

Then, of course, I had to wake Shorty up and tell him the whole story. He was so upset, I thought he was going to cry. "We need to tell the authorities," he said finally. "It's time to face the music."

Well, I'm the one who talked him out of that. "Let's not be hasty," I told Shorty. "First let's try to find where the beanstalk came up, and make sure Jack chopped it down." We thought surely he would cut it, after stealing the money, so no one could come down after him.

We searched the woods for days. We looked again at that hole under the roots of the fallen tree, and we found a deep gully washed out by a long-ago stream. There was no sign that a beanstalk had ever grown through in either place.

All we could do was hope that Jack had been scared enough to chop down the beanstalk and that would be the end of it. Losing the money, Shorty said, was a fair enough punishment for his carelessness. Our carelessness, I kept telling him, but he wouldn't have it and said it was all his own fault, which was just like the man, bless his kind heart.

Well, six months or more went by, and we had pretty much put the whole thing behind us. Then one morning there was a knock at the door, and when I opened it, who should be standing there, as bold as brass, but Jack himself. Oh, he looked a lot different from the skinny boy who had come the first time. He was lots taller—more than waist high to me—and he was wearing flashy new clothes, with a gold chain around his neck. His shoulders were wide and his arms that had been so skinny were bulging with muscles. I could tell right away that he'd been eating beans, and I just wanted to shake him for being so stupid.

I recognized him right away, of course, but I pretended not to. He told me his name was John this time, and gave me a story about having come up from the Downlands to visit and going for a walk and getting lost, and could he come in for a drink of water. I invited him in and gave him some lemonade. Shorty had just gone down the road to the neighbors, so I knew he'd be back before long. I figured this time we could hold Jack long enough to turn him in to Bean Control or Immigration.

Jack sat at the kitchen table—I didn't have to help him into the chair this time—just as cool as could be, and after a little chitchat, he got down to business. "That's quite a garden you have," he said. "Especially the beans. I do a little gardening myself, and I've never seen beans so healthy as yours. What's your secret?"

"Oh it's my husband who's the gardener," I said. At that Jack looked a little nervous, so he must have believed our story about Shorty eating Downlander boys. I decided to use it again. "He'll be home pretty soon, so you could ask him. Too bad it wouldn't be safe."

Now he really looked nervous. "My husband eats Downlanders, you see. Especially boys. You're a bit big—he prefers littler ones because they're tender—but cooked slow in the oven with the right seasonings, I reckon you'd do well enough. I'd hate to have to do it, of course, but if he told me to I wouldn't have any choice. I don't dare say no to him, especially when he's hungry."

It gave me a wicked satisfaction to see the sweat pop out on his forehead. "Maybe I should just be going," he said, "I could slip out through the garden."

Of course I knew he was hoping to steal some beans. "Oh, that wouldn't be a good idea," I told him. "He'd be sure to see you."

Just then I heard Shorty at the front door. I jumped up. "Oh, no! Here he is! You have to hide!"

I hustled him out the back door onto the porch. "Quick! Behind the chicken cage!" I shoved him behind the cage with Shorty's pet chicken in it, into the corner where the coats hung, and threw an old jacket of Shorty's over him.

This disturbed the hen, of course, and she squawked and fluttered. Then she laid a golden egg.

Oh, damn, I thought. *Why now?*

It wasn't real gold, of course. Well, not much, anyway. Shorty had been experimenting for weeks, trying to get the hen to lay different colored eggs by feeding her different things. He tried beets for red-shelled eggs, which sort of worked, and dandelion blooms for yellow ones, which didn't. He had high hopes for chocolate-covered eggs, but they just came out kind of a muddy tan color, and I finally made him stop wasting good chocolate on a chicken.

Then a few days earlier he started feeding the hen teeny tiny bits of real gold filed off of an old dental bridge he'd got at an auction years ago. So of course the dumb cluck of a chicken picked the worst possible time to lay a perfect gilded egg. Somebody who didn't know any better might have thought it was solid gold.

But the golden egg would just have to wait until we got rid of Jack. I rushed back into the kitchen just as Shorty came in. "Jack is back," I whispered. "You need to scare him again."

He caught on right away. "Fee, fie, fo, fum!" he shouted, making his voice all deep and scary. "I smell the blood of an

Englishman! Be he alive or be he dead, I'll grind his bones to make my bread!"

Then he went roaring around the kitchen, upsetting pots and slamming cupboard doors and shouting, "Where is he? I know he's hiding somewhere!"

After a few minutes of this, I figured it was time for Shorty to grab Jack while I called Bean Control. So I took him out to the porch and pointed to where I'd hidden Jack.

But he was gone. So were the hen and the golden egg.

We hurried outside, and ran down the road in opposite directions, but we were too late. We should have still called the cops, of course, but we didn't have any idea which way Jack had gone. And we figured, with the hen and all, they probably wouldn't believe us anyway.

Shorty was sorry he hadn't seen the golden egg, but we laughed and laughed at the thought of Jack climbing all the way down the beanstalk with that hen under his arm, only to find out she didn't lay real golden eggs at all. After that we spent several days searching the woods again, but we never found the beanstalk.

It was only a few weeks later when Jack came back the third time. I was out in the garden when he came in at the gate just like he owned the place. He must have been eating lots of beans in the meantime. He wasn't much taller, but his arm muscles practically bulged right out of his expensive silk shirt, and his face was all freckled with that pigment change the beans cause in some people. Both his arms had tattoos of bean vines that wrapped around from his wrists to above his elbows. But it was his manner that had changed the most. His eyes had a wild look, and he kept glancing back and forth like he was expecting somebody to sneak up on him, and he jumped at the least little sound. I tell you, I was scared of him.

And that was before I saw the gun in his hand. He poked the barrel of that pistol into my belly, and backed me right up to the garden bench. He shouted "Sit!" and I sat. Quick as could be, he ran around behind me and shoved the gun barrel up against the back of my head. I've never been so terrified in my life.

Shorty was sitting on the porch swing, tuning his harp. That harp was one of his prized possessions. Bought it at an estate sale, he did, so battered and dusty it looked like a piece of junk. But he cleaned it and fixed it up and put new electronics in, and it worked better than new. He had programmed it so he just had to say, "Play, harp," for it to start, and it made the most beautiful music you can imagine. We had it play at the funeral—Shorty would have loved that.

Jack stood there with the gun pressed to my head, and he shouted, "I got your wife, Mr. Magic Bean Man! Get out here!"

Shorty came charging out into the garden, with the harp still in his hand. "That's far enough!" Jack shouted. "One step closer, and your big fat wife is a goner."

Shorty stopped; I'd never seen his face so white. "What do you want?" he asked.

"What do you think, you big dumb shit? Beans." Jack threw a big tote bag toward him. "Go fill that sack. I want every bean in your garden, and I want them now!"

Shorty put the harp down on the patio table. His hands were shaking so hard it took him three tries to pick up the bag. "Okay, okay," he said, and I could tell he was trying to sound calm. "You can have all the beans you want. Just don't hurt my wife."

All the time Shorty was picking beans, Jack kept the gun to my head, and he kept talking. Mostly to himself, I think. "I'll have enough plants to be the biggest dealer in the country. Nobody's going to call me 'poor Jack' then. I'll show them."

I hardly dared to breathe. I'd seen enough videos about Downlanders going crazy on beans to know how dangerous Jack was. There was no telling what he might do even after he got his hands on the beans. And in the background, the whole time, the harp kept singing. Somehow, hearing that beautiful music made everything worse.

It didn't help, either, to know that none of the beans were ripe yet. No matter where Jack planted them, they weren't going to grow. Once he realized that, I figured, he would be back.

About the time I started to think I couldn't take it for one more minute, Shorty picked the last bean. He held up the sack to show Jack it was almost full. "Here's your beans. Now let my wife go."

"Not so fast," Jack said. "First, put the harp in the bag."

Shorty did. Even muffled inside the bag, the music was lovely.

"Now, we're all going to take a little walk to the beanstalk," Jack said. "Nice and slow. You go first, Mr. Bean Man, and carry the bag. If I even think you're going to try anything, wifey here gets it in the guts."

Well, that scared me so bad I could hardly stand up. My legs felt so wobbly I wasn't sure they would hold me. But Jack marched us all into the woods, with Shorty in front and me following, and Jack behind me with the gun. Every time I stumbled or hesitated, he poked me in the back with it. And all the time he kept shouting directions at us, steering us where he wanted us to go.

When he finally yelled "Stop!" we were at the uprooted tree Shorty and I had found when we were searching for the beanstalk. The base of the tree, a tangle of dry roots up on end, was higher than my head. The hollow under it, where Shorty and I had dug looking for a hole, was half-filled with loose dirt and dried leaves.

With the hand that wasn't holding the gun in my back, Jack motioned for Shorty to get down into the hollow. "There," he said. "Grab that root and pull on it."

Shorty did, and a section of the roots came open, almost like a door. There, hidden under the trunk of the tree, was the hole. I could just see the cut-off end of the beanstalk. Jack must have kept it trimmed back.

"Put the bag down beside the hole," Jack said, and Shorty did. "Now get on over there by that tree." He pointed at one a little ways away. When Shorty hesitated, Jack poked me with the gun so hard I let out a sort of gasp. "Move it! Or I'll shoot her."

Shorty moved it, though I could see how much he hated to.

"Now put your arms around the tree, as high as you can reach." Jack was shouting practically in my ear, and I could feel the gun shaking in his hand. I didn't think it was possible to get more terrified than I was already, but I did. "Now you," he said to me. "On the ground. Face down. Look away from me."

I laid down as quick as I could.

"Hands behind your back!"

I lay there, dry leaves tickling my nose so I was afraid I would sneeze and give Jack an excuse to do something drastic. I could hear him grunt as he picked up the heavy sack. The harp sang out a long, sad note, almost like it was saying goodbye. I'll hear that sound in my heart till my dying day.

Then I heard a scrambling noise, like Jack was crawling down into the hole. And suddenly there was a shot, and Shorty yelled, and I couldn't help it, I let out a shriek. That was about as awful as anything—I thought Shorty was shot, and he thought I was, and by the time we figured out we were both okay, of course Jack was gone.

And right then we made the worse mistake of all the mistakes we made in this whole sorry mess. I wanted us both to go for the police right away, but Shorty insisted he had to go down the beanstalk. "You get the cops," he said, "I'm going after him." He gave me a quick kiss and squeezed himself down into the hole, and that's the last time I saw him alive.

Well, you know the rest. How Jack chopped down the beanstalk while Shorty was still climbing down, and how he fell. The doctors said he was killed instantly, which is a little bit of comfort.

I know it was the beans that made Jack do it. I know he needs rehab for his addiction, and I suppose he'll get that while he's in prison. I can even believe he didn't kill Shorty on purpose. But two things really upset me. One is that his prison sentence is for bean dealing, not for killing my husband. The prosecutors didn't even charge him with murder.

And what's even worse is the way the Downlander media is making Jack out to be the victim, or even some sort of a hero. "Jack the Giant Killer," they call him, like it's something to be proud of.

I just want people to know the whole truth. That Jack was a thief and a bean dealer, and he killed my husband, who was the sweetest man who ever lived. At least, in prison, Jack had to go off the beans cold turkey. I hear the withdrawal takes a long time. I hope it's been really painful.

The Fairest Queen of All

The Fairest Queen of All

Thank goodness for the magic mirror; I don't think I could have managed without it. It couldn't help me deal with Snow White, but at least it simplified the other major challenge of being a queen: looking fabulous.

Let's face it, looking beautiful is what princesses and queens do. Nobody wants to know what we think; nobody cares how we feel. They just expect us to show up for their coming-out parties or parades or supermarket openings, looking our best and smiling graciously while we accept flowers from little girls and coo at babies.

The "smiling graciously" part can be a bit hard if you're having the kind of day when you'd really have preferred to stay in bed with a good book, but usually people are so pleasant that it's rather fun. Looking fabulous day in and day out, though, is a chore.

This is where the magic mirror comes in. It's been in the family for so many generations that no one really remembers where it came from. Supposedly my several-times-great-grandmother got it from an old witch in exchange for some favor or other—giving the witch her first-born child or something equally gothic, I suppose. But for all we know, some ancestor bought it at a flea market or found it in an attic or even stole it.

We do know two things. One, the mirror only responds to one person at a time. It can only be passed on to another queen or princess in the family, either by the current user or by the mirror's own choice. Two, the thing really is magic. It's possessed, or occupied, or whatever you want to call it, by an entity with a perfect fashion sense. The entity is clearly male, though he's never told any of us his name and doesn't seem to care what we call him. My mother was so grateful for his help that she called him the Divine Mr. M. I think of him as MM, which seems friendlier, not to mention shorter.

No matter what its secret is, the mirror is really quite practical and a great help. Mother gave it to me when married my dear Lionel and became a queen, and I quickly learned to rely on it. Every morning I would ask it the ritual question, just the way my mother and grandmother had taught me: "Mirror, mirror, on the wall; who is the fairest of them all?"

And the mirror would always answer, "Truly I tell you, oh my queen; you're the fairest to be seen."

Of course it's gratifying to be told you're the fairest one of all. But while that answer might be flattering, it's not all that useful. This is where the mirror was invaluable. After the ritual of that opening exchange, he would settle down to specific feedback. Like, "Oh, sweetie, that hairstyle is way too poufy for the shape of your face. Your Great-Great-Aunt Beatrice is the only one I've ever seen who could get by with that look." Or, "That blouse is a lovely shade of rose, but don't you think the purple jacket with it is just a little too kindergartenish?" Or, "Wherever did you get that cashmere? It's perfect! Just the right blend of casual friendliness and royal dignity."

MM was always good about answering specific questions, too. And the thing that I appreciated most was his ability to tell the truth with tact. One of the most important things I learned from him was to trust my own fashion instincts. For example, if I have to ask a question like, "Does this color really work for me?" I already know that the answer is no.

So with his help, I learned to show up for each day of royal duties, looking appropriately fabulous. It was a great comfort, when I left my childhood kingdom behind, to know I would have MM's help and support in my new home.

I didn't realize the toughest challenge I would face was something he couldn't help me with: Snow White.

From the beginning, I did the best I could to be as fair as I knew how and to make friends with her. Poor little thing, she lost her mother when she was just a baby. I thought I could make it up to her. I thought in time she would learn to love me. I imagined us bonding over shopping trips and little-girl tea parties, and enjoying private family dinners with the king, and having the kind of intimate conversations I had with my own mother. I can't believe how naïve I was.

Snow White was a beautiful child, and really quite sweet. But stubborn—you cannot believe how stubborn she could be when she set her mind to something. I tried to get her interested in ballet lessons. What princess doesn't take ballet, after all? She absolutely refused. She wanted to play soccer instead. At first her father said no to that—he didn't want his royal daughter out there getting kicked in the shins like any commoner's child.

I was the one who persuaded him to change his mind and let her play. I even went to all her games. Her father was so busy he only got to a few of them, but I made sure to be there, sitting in the bleachers for hours and cheering her on. My security people hated that, of course, and my maid was horrified. She scolded me for going out in public without dressing up, and fussed over what the wind and sun could do to my complexion, and was appalled when I started wearing a baseball cap. But MM said I looked great in jeans and the cap was cute as long as I tilted it just right. And most of the time, I actually enjoyed myself. It was fun to sit in the bleachers and talk to regular people and feel ordinary for a change. As a bonus, the media loved it, and the royal family's approval ratings went up several points.

It wasn't exactly how I had imagined bonding with Snow White, but it did help bring us closer together. She still didn't fully accept me, but she stopped glaring at me across the dinner table and telling me, "I don't have to do what you say; you might be the queen, but you're not my mother." We began to have some pleasant conversations and even started to do a few fun things together. I thought we were becoming friends.

Then she became a teenager.

Now, I get it, really I do. Adolescence is tough. And being a royal teenager is—let's face it—a royal pain. I've been there. I remember how awful it was. You can't have acne or flunk an algebra test or even roll your eyes at your parents in public without some gossip columnist blabbing it to the whole world. You miss out on school trips and dating and proms and all the other ordinary things that ordinary kids get to do, either because you have tutors instead of going to real school, or because security says you can't go. Even if you do get to show up at a dance or something, most guys are afraid to even talk to you. And the very idea of a first kiss or anything romantic is just a bad joke, with two or three security guys practically breathing down your neck every minute.

So I knew what Snow White was going through, and I would have loved to talk with her about it and help her. But she wouldn't let me. She pushed me as far away as she could, and it was only a small comfort to know she did the same thing with her father.

We thought it would help when her father let her go to school outside the palace. Not so much. She was so rude to the children of aristocrats who had been her friends that most of them refused to visit. But then she would bring home these really sleazy friends from school and expect us to give them a royal welcome. She would sneak out after curfew to see them, she started smoking on the sly, and once I caught her lowering a bucket down outside the castle walls to smuggle in cheap beer. And don't even get me started on the tattoo. Thank goodness, it was just a dainty little rose on her hip instead of a dragon curling down her arm or something—at least she had that much sense. I would never say this to her father, but I actually thought it was kind of cute. But that wasn't really the point. The real reason we were so upset about it was that she didn't even try to get permission; she just forged her father's signature on the parental consent form.

All in all, Snow White's teenage years seemed like one long audition for a bad movie titled, "I Was an Evil Teenage Vampire Princess." Somehow, though, we all managed to muddle through most of her adolescence without too much drama other than the occasional nasty headline or embarrassing photograph in one of the tabloids.

Then came Snow White's 18th birthday. We held the obligatory public party, which at her request was an afternoon picnic on the castle grounds with all the guests asked to bring gifts for the city's homeless children instead of her. It was a thoughtful royal gesture, and both her father and I praised and thanked her for it. We went to bed that night hoping perhaps the worst was over and she was beginning to grow up.

Then came the awful next morning. As I was dressing for the day, I asked MM as usual: "Mirror, mirror, on the wall; who is the fairest of them all?"

And he said, "You are fair enough, it's true; but Snow White is fairer now than you."

I stared into the mirror in shock for a moment, and then I just lost it. I'm embarrassed to admit it, but I threw a plain, old-fashioned hissy fit. Honestly, I wasn't upset because MM said Snow White was more beautiful than me. After all, I knew that already. I'm definitely pretty, with a good figure and even features and nice hair and interesting hazel eyes. But Snow White is a true beauty. It's more than just the contrast of her fair skin with her brown eyes and all that glossy black hair. She has perfect features, and a fantastic smile when she bothers to use it, and the kind of good bones that will make her look elegant even when she's 90.

No, the real reason was entirely different. You see, she had shown up at her birthday party with her hair dyed a dreadful yellowish green. She had on black nail polish, black lipstick, and black eye shadow. She was wearing a studded leather dog collar, torn jeans, and a ragged black tee-shirt decorated with a skull and crossbones and held together with big safety pins. And this was what the magic mirror thought was the fairest in the land? I ask you!

So yes, I did some shouting. I don't even remember what all I said, but by the time I was done the magic mirror had turned a dark smoky gray. Finally, when I ran out of breath and vocabulary, MM managed to get my attention. In a soft tone that was much kinder than I deserved, he said, "My dearest queen, you're absolutely right. And I'm sorry to leave you. But don't you see? You have learned everything I have to teach you; you're a lovely woman who always looks every inch a queen. And now Snow White needs my help."

His gentleness just made me burst into tears. After I cried myself out, and took a few minutes to practice the calming breaths my yoga trainer recommends so I could pull myself together, I had to admit MM was right. I apologized for my bad behavior and did my best to thank him for everything he had done for me. Trying not to whine in a way unbecoming to a queen, I said, "But Snow White won't even want your help, will she?"

"Not right now," he agreed. "But when she does—and based on my experience, my dear, she will before long—I'll be there for her."

I couldn't argue with that, so I sucked it up and remembered one of my mother's admonitions: "Royalty Equals Responsibility." I told MM goodbye with as much composure as I could manage, and when his image disappeared I picked up the mirror and carried it down to Snow White's bedroom to give it to her.

She didn't want it.

Not only that, but she rejected it with scorn and downright rudeness. I don't remember everything she said, but she used a lot of words like "shallow" and "vain" and "self-centered." Given how hard I had worked to be a good stepmother to her as well as a good queen, it was too much. I lost it again. I said things I regret. Snow White said things she ought to regret. None of it was at all pretty, and there was crying and shouting on both sides. I finally dumped the mirror on her bed and stormed out of her room in tears.

She didn't come down to lunch or dinner, which frankly was just fine with me. I sent trays up to her room, and her father and I agreed we would talk with her the next day when everyone had calmed down.

Except the next morning, she was gone.

We tried to keep it quiet, of course, hoping we would find her before the media was all over the story. The king met with the security people and got a search started immediately, while I called all of her friends I knew about. We had to consider the possibility that she had been kidnapped, of course, even though we were almost certain she had run away from home.

But the day went by, and then a second one, and we still hadn't found her. Then the so-called huntsman got wind of her disappearance somehow, and he went to the media.

Which would have been bad enough, but even worse, everything he told them was an outright lie. What really happened was that just a few weeks earlier we had found out he wasn't a huntsman at all. He was a member of a radical animal-rights group who had infiltrated the castle. He let a whole flock of peacocks loose in the banquet room, and he poured paint on three of my fur coats, and I don't know what all else. He was lucky we just fired him and didn't press charges.

Still, when Snow White went missing, he saw his chance. The next thing we knew, the tabloids came out with blazing red headlines: "Snow White's Escape from Toxic Palace Life!" "Brave Huntsman Refuses to Harm Princess!" "'Bring Me Her Heart,' Screams Wicked Queen!"

Even some of the mainstream media was quick to join in. In all the uproar, nobody paid much attention to the handful of stories that pointed out the truth. The lies made a better story and sold more advertising. It was disgusting and hurtful, and it was the last thing we needed when the king and I were already worried sick.

It was three more days before we finally found her. She was living in a grubby little cottage in the forest—with seven men! Seven filthy, hairy, ugly, old, little men. She was cooking and cleaning for them just like a kitchen maid, and claiming to be happy. They needed her, she said.

Her father—and believe me, I respect the man for this—decided to do the tough love thing and just leave her there for a while. He figured the cooking and cleaning would get old in a hurry. Now, I knew he was right and supported him every inch of the way, especially since I knew the security people were keeping an eye on her. But I couldn't stop worrying. Finally I couldn't stand it any more. I disguised myself as a ragged old woman selling apples, and I went out there to see how she was.

Poor little Snow White looked awful—way too thin, with her hands all rough and red, her dress torn and dirty, and her hair not even washed. I just about cried. She asked me in as if she were glad to see a friendly face, and I sat down to peel an apple for her. She took one bite, and the next thing I know she fainted—passed out right there on the floor. It might have been just hunger and overwork, but I think there was something more. There were seven funny-looking pipes in a row by the fireplace. Who knows what those disgusting little men might have been smoking?

But anyway, there I was down on the floor, slapping her face to try to bring her around, and I was in such a dither that I still had the paring knife in my hand, so I suppose maybe it really didn't look too good to the prince who was riding by and happened to look in the window.

Of course, we didn't know he was a prince right then. I just knew that this handsome young man came bursting through the door, shoved me out of the way, grabbed Snow White up in his arms, and shouted, "Don't you hurt her!"

She woke up then. Who wouldn't, with that much commotion? She looked into his eyes and he looked into hers, and I could see that it was all over but the explanations and it was time to start planning a royal wedding.

I knew Snow White was really growing up when she was the first one to apologize. Of course I apologized, too, for my part in the whole mess, and we both cried and hugged each other, and for the first time it felt like we were family.

She was more than ready to come home, even though she insisted on waiting till the seven ugly little men came home so she could tell them goodbye. They were downright cross about losing their housemaid, and only two of them even had the decency to thank Snow White for all her hard work.

She invited them to the wedding anyway. At least Maximilian—that's the prince, and no, he doesn't like to be called Max for short—managed to talk her out of having all seven of them in the wedding party. He said he had obligations to his cousins. They did behave well enough through the ceremony, and I think the rest of the guests were entertained by the dance they did at the reception.

Show White and I had fun together planning the wedding, and of course she was a beautiful bride. Once we got past that first little misunderstanding, Maximilian and I have gotten along very well. He's just the sort of young man you hope your daughter falls in love with: responsible and kind and sensible, not to mention wise enough to love Snow White for her inner beauty and not just her looks. It's a plus, too, that his land adjoins ours and the two kingdoms are longtime allies.

And finally, now that she's running a castle of her own, Snow White is really becoming the daughter and friend I always hoped she would be. We text and talk to each other practically every day. She's even started to ask me for advice about managing the household budget and receiving visiting dignitaries and that sort of thing.

One thing she doesn't ask me is about fashion. She has MM for that, and a good thing too, since right now she doesn't have much time to worry about her appearance. Even though in my opinion Snow White is lovelier than ever, and even though MM still calls her the fairest in the land, she and I both know better. That title has passed on to a new princess.

My sweet, adorable, incredibly beautiful and absolutely perfect new granddaughter.

Would you like to see some pictures?

The Determined Mama Bear

The Determined Mama Bear

Statement of Mrs. Ursula Brown (*Ursus arctos*), as recorded during a home visit by social workers Arabella Dawson (*Corvus brachyrhynchos*) and Michelle Anderson (*Homo sapiens*) in the matter of the adoption application for the minor child Goldie Locke (*Homo sapiens*), pursuant to the Interspecies Adoption Child Protection Act (IACPA).

Poor little Goldie; everyone in our part of the forest knew about her. Ran wild, she did. Out in the woods by herself, all hours of the day, when she should have been safe at home. And her not even old enough to be in school yet. Only a little older than my Baby. Brandon, I mean—he hates it when I forget and still call him Baby.

Oh, I'm sure Goldie's parents have plenty of problems of their own. Usually I'm not one to judge people if I haven't walked a mile in their paw prints, as the saying goes. But I don't care what their issues were—it was no excuse for neglecting that sweet little girl the way they did.

Even as dirty as she always was then, Goldie was a pretty little thing. Those bright blue eyes were just huge in her little face, she was so thin and so pale. And of course she had that lovely golden hair—what you could see of it through the dirt and tangles. Nothing like the soft, shiny curls she has now.

We'd see her every now and again, hiding in the trees near our house or behind the beehives. Max and I always smiled and said hi, and Baby—er, Brandon always wanted her to come into the yard and play. But the minute she saw that we knew she was there, off into the trees she went.

Then one day, Brandon was out in the yard, carrying a biscuit with honey. It's his very favorite snack, and he was taking it out to his little playhouse under the maple tree. I was up on the porch, just about to go back into the house, when I saw him run over to the fence. And there, peeking through it, was Goldie. I stayed still, not wanting to scare her off, you know. It was so cute, those two little ones looking at each other through the fence. Then Baby held out his paw, and I saw he was offering her his biscuit. I have to tell you, my heart just melted like warm honey. It was so sweet of him.

She looked at him for a minute, like she couldn't quite believe her eyes, and then she took the biscuit. She took a bite, and gave him this big smile like it was the best thing she had ever tasted. Then she looked up and saw me watching, and off she ran.

It was only about a week later that her visit happened. And I don't care what the human attorney for the Lockes called it in her IACPA brief—it was a visit, not a "kidnapping." I try not to take that personally; I know lawyers have to do their jobs. And I do know there's plenty of foolishness and stereotyping on both sides. Like that silly crow—no offense meant, Miss Dawson, but that bird is an embarrassment to her species—anyway, she's always ranting on that anti-human blog she calls "Take Back The Wild," and she called Goldie's visit a "home invasion," of all things. To us, it's just Goldie's first visit. I probably shouldn't say this, but in my heart I think of it as Goldie's homecoming.

Here's what happened: It was a beautiful summer morning, and we were all up early. While I was making breakfast, Max took Brandon and went out to the sweet clover patch to start the sprinkler. He likes to water early in the morning, and he pays special attention to the clover because it's so important for the honey bees.

Getting the sprinkler going usually only takes a few minutes, so while the coffee was brewing I went ahead and dished up the porridge. It's my own recipe—organic steel-cut oats mixed with wheat berries and flax seed. After it's cooked I mix in some peanut butter, plus some of our own honey, of course. I filled Brandon's bowl, added a little milk, and set it on the table to cool. I put lots of milk on mine, because I like it lukewarm. And Max's I stuck in the microwave for an extra 45 seconds—he prefers his without milk, and eats it so hot I don't see how he doesn't burn his tongue.

I had just set Max's bowl on the table when I heard the commotion outside. I dropped the potholder and ran out to see what was wrong. Brandon was crying, but in an odd sort of smothered way, and it sounded like Max was laughing, of all things.

Well, while Max was busy with the hose, Brandon climbed up one of the big oak trees, crawled out on a big branch, and jumped down on top of one of the bee hives. Somehow when he landed, he knocked the lid off and fell right into the hive. Head-first.

Now I know that lawyer is trying to use this to make out that Max and I are negligent and careless and I don't know what all. As if letting a bear cub climb trees is risky, for goodness sakes. Or as if one little mishap, with no harm done but a good lesson learned, makes anyone a bad parent. If they want to talk about bad parenting, why don't they look at people who let their little girl run wild, and don't even keep her clean or make sure she has enough to eat.

I've even heard claims from the Lockes that keeping bees makes our household a dangerous place for children. What nonsense! From the time Brandon was old enough to be outside we've taught him to respect the bees—to move quietly, and treat them gently, and leave them in peace to make the honey that he likes so much.

Well, he certainly got enough of it that morning. By the time I got there Max had grabbed his feet and hauled him out of the hive. There he was, hanging upside down, licking honey off of his paws. His face was all covered, and his fur was sticky, and he had honey dripping from his ears. He certainly wasn't crying any more—the little rascal looked so pleased with himself it was downright laughable. He'd have been a perfect poster child for that saying, "Happy as a bear in honey." But of course you've probably seen the pictures on Facebook. Max put them up with the title, "Brandon's high-five hive dive."

Well, the bees were already lighting on him, because of course they wanted to reclaim the honey and put it back in the comb. Max and I decided it would be a good lesson for Brandon to sit and wait while the bees did their work. So we parked him on the picnic table and told him a couple of stories to keep him still while the bees cleaned the honey off of his fur. It was amazing how quick they were and how clean he was when they were done. Except for what he had licked up himself, they got every drop of that honey and flew back to the hive with it.

The only damage to our little honey-hunter was one sting on his nose, which happened when he first fell into the hive and surprised the bees. And that was a good thing, because it helped Brandon remember why it's important to respect them.

By the time the bees were finished, of course we were all really hungry, so we headed for the house to have our breakfast. And that's when we first discovered someone had been inside.

I had put our porridge bowls on the table in our own places, with the spoons and napkins beside them. Now all our chairs were pulled out, and the bowls were all out of place. Max's spoon was beside his plate in a splatter of porridge, looking like someone had dropped it. Mine had the spoon in it. And Brandon's special little matching bowl and spoon that his grandma had sent him was completely empty. Poor baby, he looked at it with big sad eyes and said, "Mama, somebody's been eating our porridge—and they ate mine all up!"

Honestly, when I saw the empty bowl I had a fair idea who had slipped into the house while we were outside. But I didn't say anything yet. I picked up my bowl to put it into the microwave and warm it up for Brandon, but while I was doing that he ran into the living room. "Oh, no, Papa—come look!" he shouted. "Somebody's been sitting in our chairs. And they broke mine all to pieces!"

Max and I both hurried in to see. There was Baby, sitting on the floor by the little wooden chair Max made for him. The chair was tipped on its side, and he was holding up one leg—the chair's leg, I mean, not his. He wasn't crying or anything, just very serious the way little ones can get, and he told Max, "Look, Papa, you need to fix it." Of course he thinks his father can fix anything—which isn't far from the truth, really.

Max took the leg and picked up the chair. "You're right," he told Brandon. "I need to fix it. See here? The leg came off. Just a little glue, and it will be good as new."

"But, Papa," Brandon asked him, "Who broke it? Who was in our house? And where did they go?"

Max looked at me, and I looked at Max, and it was pretty clear we were thinking the same thing. "Let's look upstairs," I said.

So we tiptoed up the steps. First we peeked into the master bedroom. Max's pillow—he has this old ratty thing that's hard as a plank, but he says that's how he likes it—had been moved. My nice soft pillow had a dent in it from someone's head, and I thought I saw a blonde hair on it.

Max and I started for Brandon's room, but he was ahead of us. "Somebody's been sleeping in our beds," he cried. "And look—here she is!"

Just as we suspected, it was Goldie. She was curled up in his bed, cozy as could be, just like she belonged there.

Of course Brandon's shouting woke her up. She opened her eyes, saw us leaning over her, and burst into tears. I know the attorney is going to say it was because she was scared of us. But I know better. I remember every word she said, because it went straight to my heart. She reached up her little hands to me and said, "I'm sorry! I didn't mean to break the chair—it just broke. I won't do it ever again, I promise! Please don't let them hit me!"

Well, what would any mother have done? I picked her up out of that bed and sat down in the rocking chair and cuddled her. Brandon ran and got one of his favorite stuffed toys, a soft little elephant, and tucked it right into her arms. She held onto that with one arm, and clutched my fur with her other hand like she never wanted to let go, and she just cried and cried. I snuggled her close and sang to her and let her cry herself out. Max sat on the bed and held Brandon, who kept leaning over to pat Goldie on the foot, since that was the only part of her he could reach.

When she was about calmed down, I whispered to Max that he should take Brandon downstairs and give him his breakfast. Poor baby, he must have been starving by then.

Well, quiet as I was, Goldie heard me, and that set her off again. "Oh, no—I was bad! I ate up all his breakfast. I'm sorry! I only meant to have a taste."

It took me a while to convince her that we had plenty of porridge and Brandon wasn't going to go hungry. I finally took her downstairs and showed her the big plastic container we keep the dry porridge in, and I let her help me make some more. Poor little one, she had two more bowls of it before she was full. Then I gave her a bath, and dressed her in some of Brandon's clothes, and combed out her hair. While I was working the tangles out of her curls, she said, sounding surprised, "It doesn't even hurt. I never knew you could comb hair without hurting." That made me want to cry. By the time we were done she was yawning, and she fell asleep in my lap, and while I sat there holding her I vowed I would do whatever it took to keep her with us and give her the love and care she deserved.

Max and I talked it over while she was sleeping, and he agreed with me all the way. But of course we knew we couldn't just keep her, much as we wanted to. That's when we called Child Protection Services and started this whole process.

And I have to say, we were a little surprised—oh, we were thrilled about it, don't think we weren't—but surprised, too, at how smoothly it's gone so far. Even with all the paperwork and home visits and background checks and everything, getting approved as foster parents for Goldie was a lot easier than we expected. And if being her foster parents is the best we can get, why, we'll take that and be happy. But we'd love to be able to adopt her, and have her grow up knowing we're really her family and no one is going to take her away.

I do get it that mostly it makes sense for young ones to grow up with their own species. But I also believe, right down to my hind claws, that the more we all get to know and understand each other the better we can all get along. We've already seen that for ourselves since we've had Goldie. We're getting acquainted with lots more of our neighbors, humans and everybody.

We take her to the Ten Little Fingers preschool, where most of the children are human, so she'll have plenty of interaction with her own species. Goldie loves it there. I think some of the other parents were a bit nervous around Max and me at first, but they seem just fine now that we know each other better. I volunteer there once a week, and sometimes a couple of the other moms and I go out for lunch afterward. All the little ones like it when I read to them—sometimes so many of them crowd onto my lap that I can hardly see the book. They especially seem to like Goldie's favorite story, *Grizelda and the Three Little Humans*; they giggle and giggle when I do the children's voices.

We hope Goldie and Brandon both will grow up understanding that, four-legged or two, furred or feathered or bare, all of us are just people. But of course, no matter how high-minded and important all that might be, what matters most is how much we love Goldie and she loves us. She's so happy here. It's such a change from the dirty, hungry child who used to peek through our fence like a lost little wild thing.

Just the other morning, she and Brandon were at the table eating breakfast while I was at the counter mixing up a batch of honey cakes. They were chattering away, you know, like little ones do. And she gave a great big sigh, as contented as a bee in clover, and said, "Oh, Brandon, it's so nice here. Everything is just right!"

The
Softhearted
Stepsister

The Softhearted Stepsister

"Oh, my God! That's Cinderella!"

I had been paying more attention to my sociology homework than the evening news, but Jane's shriek made me drop my book and focus on the television.

A hunky young reporter with perfect hair and gleaming teeth was in the square in front of the palace, breathlessly reporting live on the latest demonstration from the anti-aristocracy group calling themselves "Unoccupy the Throne." Behind him, a few dozen people were milling around with hand-lettered signs. I saw "Down With the Crown," "Clean the House of Lords," "No Sir No More," and—quite rude, I thought—"Kingdom = Kingdumb."

The camera zoomed in on a slender girl carrying a sign so big she could barely balance it—"The Royal We Does Not Speak For Me." I could see why they chose her. Even in scruffy jeans and a baggy sweatshirt (I recognized it as the one I wore to paint the dining room last fall), Cinderella was beautiful.

"How could she?" Jane moaned. "After Papa practically died for the crown."

"Maybe that's why," Mama said softly. I glanced over and saw her smiling at the screen while tears ran down her cheeks.

"But Mama, we can't let her do this. What will people say?"

By "people," of course, Jane meant "Nigel's parents." She and her boyfriend hadn't made it official yet, but their friends, families, and everyone she had ever heard of on social media understood they planned to get married as soon as he finished law school. Nigel was the son of a baron, and his mother cared about the aristocracy and all that sort of thing.

The protesters were gone now, replaced on the screen by a line of dancing ducks singing about deodorant. Mama picked up the remote and hit mute. "We agreed Cindi needed to find something to care about, remember? Isn't this better than all that housecleaning?"

"Oh my God, yes," I said before Jane could disagree. "It was scary, the way she dusted in the corners, and cleaned the bathroom every day, and scrubbed the kitchen floor on her hands and knees when it was already clean. And remember that morning you caught her outside polishing the front steps?"

Jane said, "It was kind of handy, though, the way she organized all her clothes by color. I even started doing that myself."

Wiping her eyes, Mama gave a sort of watery laugh. "I noticed clothes on the floor in her room the other day. I never thought I'd be glad to see that."

"She still mostly wears ratty old jeans and tee-shirts, but at least Jane and I don't have to brush her hair for her and practically drag her into the shower the way we'd been doing."

I thought we were safely away from the topic of what our little sister was doing on the evening news, but I should have known Jane better than that. "I'm as glad as anybody to see Cindi less depressed. But protesting? What if she gets arrested or something?"

"Your sister is too sensible to do anything violent or outrageous."

"Sensible? Attacking the royal family is sensible? Dressing like a homeless person is sensible?"

I had to laugh. "It is, actually. Wearing those old rags is just like Cindi. It's dramatic and all that, but it's also very practical if somebody throws eggs or paint or something. Besides, she isn't exactly attacking the royal family. People complain about royalty all the time, and nobody pays much attention."

"But what if a protest gets out of hand? She could get hurt. What if this is just another form of self-destructive grief?"

I recognized the term—Psych 203, chapter six of the *Tools for Healing* textbook. I had the class last year and Jane is taking it now.

Mama never took a psychology class in her life, but she knows her daughters. "No, girls, Cindi is not trying to harm herself. She and I talk sometimes, you know, late at night when neither of us can sleep. That's been a blessing in this whole thing at least, if you can say there's such a thing as a blessing in a tragedy like this, that she and I are closer than we've ever been. I know she's done some things that seem odd. So have I, for that matter. We all have to grieve in our own way, and I truly believe she's getting through it."

"You're sure? I know this is hardest for you and Cindi, and maybe we don't understand . . ."

Jane and I grieved, certainly, when Papa was killed in that car crash. He may have been our stepfather instead of our real father, but we loved him dearly and we missed him dreadfully. But for Mama and Cinderella, it was so much worse. Their world just shattered—I mean, absolutely in pieces. Honestly, without Jane and me to look after them, I'm not sure either one would have come through it.

"I'm sure, Charlotte. This is the first thing Cindi has cared about since her father died. And if protesting against the crown brings her back to herself, we are not going to interfere." Mama's tone was one

Jane and I had learned to respect when we were little girls. There was no point in arguing.

So the next morning none of us said anything about seeing Cindi on the news, and if any of our friends recognized her, they didn't say anything, either. Honestly, with classes and homework and jobs, Jane and I were too busy to pay a lot of attention. Though Jane did write a paper on grief for her psych class; she got an A, but I noticed she didn't show it to Mama.

Over the next few weeks there were more protests, including one where the prince showed up to talk to the protesters. All the news outlets covered it, of course, and we saw our little sister on the news again. She was practically nose to nose with His Royal Highness, not shouting really, but clearly telling him exactly what she thought. Jane moaned and put her head in her hands, and even I thought Cindi was about to get arrested, but Mama gasped, "Oh, doesn't she look just like her father?" and laughed and cried at the same time.

Well, after that the protests sort of died down, and the media moved on to more exciting things. Cindi still had a couple of signs propped against the wall in her bedroom and a handful of "Unoccupy the Throne" buttons in the clutter on her dresser, but she didn't seem to be going to as many meetings or demonstrations. Instead, she started researching stuff like how much money the country spent on security for the royal family and how much the king paid in taxes and putting it up on a blog called "The Royal We Does Not Speak for Me." Personally, I thought blogging was better than compulsive cleaning, even if she still spent a lot of her time shut up in her room.

Jane and I still dragged her out every once in a while, though, when we had time to do something fun. Like the day we made her go with us to see The Fairy Godmother. It was a new store downtown— an exclusive, expensive shop for wedding dresses and ball gowns and silk suits, with a sign out front reading "Let us make magic for you." You know the kind of place, where you feel like you need to get dressed up just to go in and look around but you don't own anything quite nice enough.

We couldn't afford to shop there, of course, but one afternoon Jane begged Cindi and me to go there with her just to check it out. To drool over wedding dresses was what she really wanted, of course, but I was curious myself and even Cinderella said she wouldn't mind looking.

The place was pretty much what you'd expect—fabulous clothes displayed with understated elegance, with dainty chairs scattered here and there to sink down on if anyone felt faint after looking at the price tags. The owner was a tall, scary-slender woman with silver hair and intimidating cheekbones, but she introduced herself as Faye and was friendly and welcoming even though it was obvious we were just looking. Then after a few minutes of chitchat she offered Cinderella a part-time job. Sales clerk, shop assistant, and most important, model.

We expected her to turn it down, of course. It didn't exactly seem a good fit with "Unoccupy the Throne." But she accepted on the spot. Jane looked at me and I looked at Jane, and we kept our mouths shut tight while Cindi and Faye settled the details of salary and hours.

As soon as we got out the door, though, I grabbed Cindi by the arm. "What do you think you're doing? Don't you know who shops there? Aristos. Rich people. Minor royalty, even. I thought you hated all that."

Jane gave her Mama's best "more disappointed than angry" look. "I never though you'd be such a hypocrite."

"That's not it at all," Cindi snapped back. "I'm infiltrating. You know how women talk while they're trying on clothes; I might hear all sorts of useful things in the dressing rooms. Just think of it as an undercover assignment." She giggled at her own bad joke.

Jane didn't even crack a smile. "And I suppose you'll wear your 'Unoccupy' button?"

"Don't be silly. I'll be perfectly well-behaved, I promise. They're going to love me."

They did, too.

Cindi was good at her job, especially the modeling part. Not just because she's beautiful, which she is, even wearing ratty old jeans or just out of bed with her hair tangled. But the first time Jane and I saw our little sister in a ball gown, we were just blown away. Drifting across the room, slender and graceful, with a dreamy expression that probably meant she was eavesdropping for tidbits she could blog about, she was stunning. The wealthy women who shopped at The Fairy Godmother used words like "ethereal" and "exquisite," and they loved her.

And even more important, they loved the clothes. The Fairy Godmother was a great success, and so was Cinderella. Jane and I were incredibly proud of her. Okay, okay, so we did have a couple of conversations, just between ourselves, about the difference between her job modeling glam gowns and our jobs delivering pizza and grooming dogs. Once we started imagining trying to eat pizza without dripping grease on the fancy gowns, and comparing a few of the snooty women at the shop with the snooty dogs Jane worked on—and yes, one of us may have used the "b" word once or twice—we got the giggles and everything was fine.

Then we received the invitation to the royal ball.

The ball was an annual event, held every spring. Practically everyone in the kingdom who had enough social rank to be called "Sir So-And-So" or "Lady Whosit," or who was important in some other way, was invited. This year was an especially big deal, because the invitation list was even broader than usual. The celebrity mags and blogs were full of speculation about how it was past time Prince Edward found himself a wife.

After some very publicly unhappy marriages, followed by a couple of untidy divorces and a handful of scandals, the royal family had decided a generation back to let its children marry for love instead of political advantage. Still, a prince could be steered toward the right sort of young ladies in hopes he would fall in love appropriately, and the spring ball was part of that. Jane and I pretty much stopped looking at social media, because everybody was posting and following so much gossip about who he would choose and how he would choose and whether he would break with tradition and marry a commoner and whether he even wanted to marry at all, and it was all so gushy and romantic in a sort of medieval way that it was nauseating.

But Jane and I were still excited about getting an invitation. We decided it must have been Papa's work for the government that made us important enough to be invited. We never did know exactly what he did, except that he traveled a lot, he sometimes met with the King himself, and he never talked about his work. Jane was sure he was a spy, and she even said once—just to me, thank goodness, and I hushed her quick before Mama heard—that she didn't think the car accident that killed him was really an accident. Jane reads a lot of romantic suspense.

Why we were invited didn't really matter, of course. We had two bigger questions to deal with. First was whether Cindi would want to go. "Sure," she said with a shrug. "Faye says it will be good for business."

And second was what we were going to wear. With Mama's insurance checks, and the college funds that Papa had set up, and now all of us girls working, we got by comfortably enough. But that didn't mean the budget would cover three new ball gowns. Four, counting Mama, if we could persuade her to get one.

We had a family meeting the evening after the invitation showed up. "Maybe I could sew something," Mama offered. Jane and I looked at each other in dismay, remembering the time she tried to make me a prom dress. "Oh, no, Mama," Jane said quickly, "Four dresses at the same time would be way too much to take on."

"And it would be cheaper to get something at the second-hand shops," I added. "But I bet other people will be doing the same thing, so we need to start shopping right away."

Then Cinderella chimed in. "Oh, we don't need to do that. Faye has a plan. She needs to make sure it's okay with you, Mama, so can you all come to the shop tomorrow?"

After that, of course, we were all desperately curious, so as soon as I finished my last class the next day we dashed down to The Fairy Godmother.

Faye's plan, it turned out, was to give Mama, Jane, and me each a dress—off the clearance rack, but still way beyond what we could afford to buy—in exchange for being allowed to turn our little sister into a "mystery princess" for the ball. Cinderella would wear one of Faye's most stunning gowns, along with a matching little mask. With the mask, plus an elegant hairstyle and makeup, Faye didn't think even women who had seen her modeling at the shop would recognize her right away. She would arrive in a limo, slightly late, and make a grand entrance. Everyone would notice, everyone would gossip about it, and, of course, everyone would find out one way or another that the dress had come from The Fairy Godmother. Faye herself was not invited to the ball, but she was one of the dressers asked to be on hand in one of the upstairs dressing rooms, armed with needles, thread, and other tools of her trade to handle emergencies like torn hems or slipping straps.

At first Mama was reluctant. She didn't think using the royal ball as a marketing opportunity was quite appropriate. Faye explained how every dress shop and jewelry store in the city used it that way every year, loaning dresses and necklaces to women who would show them off. "You'd be surprised," she told Mama confidentially, "at how many duchesses don't own the diamonds they wear to special events like this."

"But while you're thinking about it," she added, "Why don't you all try on some dresses?"

That did it, of course. After Mama saw Jane in a beautiful deep blue gown that just matched her eyes and set off her curves in a totally tasteful way, she was wavering. Then she found something aqua and lacy for herself that was absolutely elegant, which was almost enough to persuade her.

When it was my turn, Cinderella zipped me into a softly draped off-one-shoulder dress in a glorious red. I would never have chosen something so dramatic, but when I looked in the mirror my jaw dropped. Looking back at me, instead of a too-tall girl with no figure, was a slender, graceful woman.

"Oh, Charly," Cindi told me, "you have to get this. It's a 'godmother gown.'"

"What's a godmother gown?"

She laughed out loud in a way she hadn't done since Papa died. Even if I hadn't already fallen in love with the dress, I'd have chosen it just because of that laugh.

"It's one that makes a girl come out of the dressing room and say, 'Oh, God, Mother, I have to have this gown!'"

We all got the dresses, of course. Faye refused to even hint at what Cindi would be wearing, though she did assure Mama it would not be too daring. "The magic of The Fairy Godmother is created with elegance and impeccable taste. That's our reputation, and Cinderella is part of it."

The idea of Cindi, whose faded tees were usually wrinkled from being tossed on the floor, as a symbol of impeccable taste was almost too much for Jane and me. By carefully not looking at each other, we did manage to stifle our giggles until we left the shop.

The night of the ball, Mama and I arrived so early it was almost embarrassing. Jane, looking like a princess in her blue gown, came in on Nigel's arm only a short time later. Nigel's parents were right behind them, his mother looking a trifle annoyed. Not enough people present to hear the master of ceremonies announce her, I thought. For Mama and me, being announced practically anonymously was just one more way to keep Cinderella's identity a secret. Not that most of the guests would recognize our names, anyway, or care if they did, but it was all part of Faye's plan.

It wasn't long until the trickle of arriving guests became a flood of glamour down the wide staircase into the ballroom. Jane and I, with some help from Nigel, made a game of trying to recognize the various debs and celebs as they were introduced, swept down the steps, and went to their neutral corners to preen with their entourages.

When the ballroom was full, and members of the orchestra were turning pages and shifting in their chairs to make the transition from background music to dance music, Cinderella appeared at the top of the stairs. If I hadn't been expecting her, I swear I wouldn't have recognized my own sister. The brown hair she usually wore pulled back into a messy ponytail was pulled up into some sort of smooth knot laced with a rope of pearls. Her gown, silver covered with lace, was deceptively simple until you noticed how it flowed and shimmered around her as she moved. Even with the upper part of her face hidden by a dainty silver mask, the woman in the dress was, not simply beautiful, but stunning. I had a hard time matching that elegant figure with the grubby, grieving little sister who had spent so many unhappy hours scrubbing in our kitchen. I felt my throat tighten with something that would have been delight if it hadn't been so close to tears, and beside me Mama clutched at my hand and took a deep breath.

"Lady Cee," the master of ceremonies intoned. (Faye had decided "Lady X" was too obvious.) The hush that followed was more than the ordinary polite pause. As Cindi came down the steps—and when had she learned to walk so gracefully in heels that high?—the crowd of society's most important and sophisticated people simply stared.

Just one person was moving. The prince himself was striding toward the steps to greet her. Cinderella stepped down from the bottom step and, without even pausing, swept into an old-fashioned curtsey that would have done credit to Marie Antoinette. The prince bowed. He offered his arm. She took it. Right on cue, the orchestra launched into the first dance of the evening, and the pair of them swept onto the floor like a couple out of a fairy tale. Everyone else watched for a few moments, and I swear I could hear the sighs even over the music—sighs of envy from every female under thirty, of disappointment from all the ambitious mamas, and of sentiment from everyone else.

Other couples started filling the dance floor, Jane and Nigel among them. I assumed my role for the evening would be to sit with Mama and watch the dancers, so I steered her toward a sofa with a good vantage point. But when the second set started, a minor lordling I had helped with chemistry class last year came over and asked me to dance. I hesitated, not wanting to leave Mama sitting alone, but she said, "Don't be silly, dear, you must," and practically shoved me out onto the floor. A short time later, I almost tripped over my partner's polished shoes when I saw Mama twirl past, smiling up at a man I recognized as one of Papa's former colleagues.

After my first partner introduced me to one of his friends, plenty of young men with no better prospects seemed pleased to dance with me. The effect of the red dress, I presumed. Since I didn't expect to see any of them again and figured they wouldn't recognize me in my usual clothes if I did, I didn't bother too much about their names.

Except one. James, a lanky redhead with unfortunate ears but deep blue eyes with a grin in them, was tall enough to make me feel almost petite. Even better, when I made some smart remark he got the joke, and he waltzed with a swooping energy that had me laughing out loud. He must have been a near-nobody, though, without enough money or status to overcome those ears, because instead of dancing with more important partners he came back to me for every waltz after we bantered our way through the first one.

Even while I was enjoying myself, I kept an eye on the rest of the family. As I expected, Jane and Nigel held each other closely while they danced except when they were whispering in secluded corners. As I expected, Mama chatted with other mature ladies and was the prettiest of any of them. As I certainly had not expected, she also danced a great many dances, and several times I caught her very nearly flirting.

And Cinderella and the prince danced together for practically the entire evening. Oh, dutiful royal son that he was, Edward did his duty by a few visiting princesses and miscellaneous daughters of dukes, but it was obvious that the only woman there who had his interest was our little sister.

All in all, it was a very satisfactory evening all the way around. At least until the midnight drama.

According to Faye's plan, Cindi was to leave the ball on the stroke of midnight. In part this was to emphasize the mystery of the "mysterious Lady Cee." In part it was because the limo company charged double after 1:00 a.m., and Faye was too careful a business woman to want the extra expense.

But Faye hadn't counted on Cindi being so enchanted with the prince that she totally lost track of the time. Of course Jane was too focused on Nigel to notice, and Mama was behaving more like a deb at her first ball than a watchful parent. So it was up to me. At five minutes to midnight, just as a waltz ended, I excused myself to James and went to pry my sister out of the prince's arms.

Not quite literally, of course. They were standing close together, not even touching, but they were smiling at each other as if they were the only two people in the room.

It was beautiful. It was touching. It was sweet.

It was four minutes to twelve.

I took a deep breath, walked right up to them, made a brief curtsy to Prince Edward, and put my hand on Cindi's arm. "I'm very sorry to interrupt you," I said—and truly, I was—"But Lady Cee absolutely must leave the ball at midnight."

"I must?" Cindi's eyes never left his face.

"She must?" He was just as bad.

"She must," I repeated, doing my best to mimic Mama's firmest tone. "There will be dire consequences if she doesn't."

Like getting fired. Like losing the job that had helped bring her out of her grief. The thought stiffened my backbone, and I took a firmer grip on her arm.

"It's three minutes to twelve, Lady Cee," I said. "You have to go. Now."

Finally she glanced at me. "Oh, yes. I must."

She didn't move, though. The prince, no fool he, took advantage of her hesitation. "Just one more dance?" he pleaded.

Cinderella wavered. I put my mouth close to her ear and hissed, "Cynthia Eleanor! Move it! Faye is waiting in the limo."

That got her full attention. "Oh, no! I do have to go. Really."

She gave the prince a look so full of fierce longing that it took my breath away. Then she bobbed a quick curtsy without her usual grace, gathered up her skirts, and whirled. She stumbled against me as she turned, jerked away from the hand I put out to catch her, and ran. It looked as if she were limping as she disappeared, and I thought she'd twisted an ankle until I saw the shoe. She had run right out of it. I bent to pick it up, but the prince scooped it up first and dashed after Cindi.

I watched him weave through the crowd, clutching the expensive silver satin pump. Three waiters, two footmen, and one of the young men I had danced with ran after him. Security, I thought; there went any thought of getting the shoe back. I hoped Faye would think the extra cost was worth it.

At least picking up the shoe had slowed the prince down enough to give Cinderella a head start. By the time he got outside, she should be safely inside the limo and disappearing into the night. Then I wondered. Had she slipped out of the shoe on purpose, for just that reason? That little practical act right in the middle of a deep romantic moment would be just like her.

Mama worked her way through the murmuring crowd to join me. "Did she get away on time?"

"Just barely."

"Thank you for making sure. I'm sorry I wasn't paying better attention; I haven't enjoyed myself so much since . . ."

Since Papa died, of course. The little spark of annoyance I had felt over being the only one keeping track of Faye's deadline instantly disappeared, and I gave her a quick hug. "I'm so glad you're having a good time. And you look so beautiful."

"So do you, Charlie dear. And obviously others agree with me."

By "others," she apparently meant James of the ears, who was approaching with the colleague of Papa's who had danced with Mama several times. Both of them had the look of men on a mission. "Their Majesties would appreciate it if everyone would resume dancing until Prince Edward returns," the older man said formally. "Would you ladies care to join us in setting a good example?"

We would, of course, having reasons of our own for smoothing over Cinderella's dramatic departure. The dancing resumed, and the prince came back, and before long he was sweeping across the floor with a stunning blonde actress in his arms for all the world as if Lady Cee hadn't just broken his heart. I had an irreverent urge to go ask him what he had done with Cindi's shoe.

In another hour or so the king and queen departed, which was the signal for nearly everyone over the age of 30 to go home and for the orchestra to switch to music actually written within the last decade. It would have been fun to stay a bit longer, as Jane and Nigel were doing, but I could see that Mama was flagging so I didn't object when she asked if I were ready to leave. James escorted us out, handed us into one of the waiting taxis just as if we were somebody important, and stood looking after us as we drove away.

Before I went to bed, I peeked in on Cindi. Her underthings were in a heap on the floor, but she had taken the time to hang up the elegant gown. She was sound asleep, with the remaining silver shoe on its side next to her pillow.

We all slept late the next morning, but Jane had just come downstairs yawning and Mama and I were on our third cups of coffee when the doorbell rang shortly before noon.

I opened the door to two identically burly men with identically bland expressions, one carrying a briefcase and the other with an enormous bouquet of red roses. Behind them, a head taller than either, was James.

"Good morning, Charl—er, Miss Spencer. I'm the Earl of Mayfeld, aide to His Royal Highness Prince Edward, and we're here on important business from the palace. May we please come in?"

It was clear that it wasn't really a question, but Mama rose graciously to the occasion and led the way to the parlor. She offered seats, made appropriate noises over the flowers as she moved my laptop to make room for them on the side table, and sent me to kitchen for coffee. All the while a part of my mind was buzzing with curiosity about the "important business," while another part was going, "*Earl? Aide to the prince?*"

The security guards pretending to be footmen perched on the edges of their chairs and accepted coffee with the air of men who seldom drank while on duty. James—*did he really say Earl?*—looked at me with gratitude as he took the cup I offered and drank half of it down like medicine. Then he nodded to the footman with the briefcase, who opened it and handed over its contents.

Cinderella's missing shoe.

James took a deep breath and launched into what seemed to be a rehearsed speech. "I am looking for the lady who lost this shoe at the ball last night. Prince Edward has instructed me to search for her, because he greatly desires her—er, desires to find her."

He turned red to the tips of his ears, so embarrassed it made me want to deflect attention from his oh-so-Freudian slip of the tongue. "Well, it certainly can't be me; I'd never fit into that shoe. See?" I wriggled a slippered foot at him. He abandoned whatever he had planned to say and turned to me.

"Charlotte, you spoke to Lady Cee just before she disappeared last night. Is she your stepsister?"

I looked at Mama. She didn't say a word. I looked at Jane. She shrugged. Feeling sorry for James or not, I kept my mouth shut.

He looked disappointed. "Okay; let's try it this way. We may seem a century or two out of date at the palace, but we do know a few things, and we do use the Internet. I know perfectly well that the woman who came to the ball as Lady Cee is really Cynthia Eleanor Lewis, called Cinderella by her family and friends. She is your stepdaughter, Mrs. Lewis, and the daughter of the late Sir Edgar Lewis, who was knighted for unspecified services to the crown. She works at an upscale dress shop called The Fairy Godmother. She has been seen at anti-royalty rallies and publishes a blog called 'The Royal We Does Not Speak for Me'—which, by the way, is really quite solidly researched and well-written.

"I realize you may not trust us, but please believe me that Cinderella is absolutely not in any kind of trouble. Quite the opposite. Edward is in love with her. Really in love, I think." One corner of his mouth quirked up in a wry smile. "And I ought to know—I've been up all night listening to him talk about her. He insists she's the only woman he will ever want to marry."

I remembered the way Cindi and the prince had looked at each other the night before. Then I thought about her blog, and the "Unoccupy the Throne" buttons on her dresser, and the way she had lectured Edward at the protest rally. "With all that listening, did you happen to hear him say anything about respecting her enough to ask whether she even cares about who he wants to marry?"

James didn't seem offended, just gave me the same grin I had found so appealing the night before. "Of course he did. That's the whole point of sending me out first thing this morning to find her."

Mama stood up, which made all three men jump to their feet as they remembered their formal manners; representatives of the crown and all that. "I'll go wake her up. Charly, will you please make another pot of coffee, and Jane, I think we have some scones in the freezer."

As we followed her out of the room, I saw James pull out his phone and start texting.

Twenty minutes later Cindi came downstairs, barefoot and with her hair wet, wearing jeans and a tee shirt that at least didn't have an anti-royal slogan on it. The second shoe dangled casually from one finger, and her attitude was all relaxed and "this is how I always look at home." I might almost have believed it if I hadn't noticed she had taken time to put on eyeliner and mascara.

When the doorbell rang just as Cindi swallowed the last of her scone, James nodded to one of the phony footman. The man leaped up, but I froze him in his tracks with a glare, shot a matching one at James, and said sweetly, "Not your house, remember? I'll get it."

Just as I expected, it was Prince Edward, with two more minions and more roses. Red and pink this time.

When Edward came into the parlor, everyone dutifully stood—except Cinderella. Not that it mattered. He was across the room in two strides, dropped to his knees in front of her, and said in true fairy-tale fashion, "Will you marry me?" It was a classic romantic moment, only slightly spoiled when he added, "I've loved you since the night we met at the protest and you called me an anachronistic leech."

Cindi blushed, and then she started to laugh, and he leaned forward and kissed her and she kissed him back.

While the rest of us were busy not staring—Jane texting Nigel as fast as her thumbs would go, and me fiddling with the yellow roses, and Mama encouraging the minions to finish off the scones—James came over to me. "I'm sorry for being high-handed a minute ago. I promise I won't make a habit of it."

"And why should that possibly matter to me?"

He turned red again, ears and all. "Because I—because you—well, because these flowers aren't for your sister. They're for you."

Before I could respond to that, Cindi came up for air and said, "But you're the prince."

"Guilty as charged. Just another 'parasite on the backs of the working poor,' if I'm quoting correctly."

"Oh, my God—you've read my blog?"

"Every post."

"He certainly has," James whispered into my ear. "All night long. Most of them out loud to his captive audience of one."

"No wonder you knew it was well-written," I whispered back without a bit of sympathy.

He grinned and squeezed my hand, which seemed to have ended up in his without my noticing. "I took notes, for counter-arguments about all the ways the royals really are useful members of society. I could take you to dinner and explain them to you."

Cindi said something that ended with "won't stop blogging."

As a member of the family, you'd have access to all sorts of inside information," Edward told her.

"And I want donations for the homeless instead of wedding presents."

"An excellent idea. Too many expensive dust-catchers in the palace already."

I looked up at James, noticing what a deep blue his eyes were, and Cindi and Edward's voices faded into the background. "It sounds like there will be arrangements to make. Someone from the family might need to meet with an aide to the prince."

"Several times, no doubt. These things can take days."

"Weeks, even." I glanced at my little sister, deep in negotiations with Prince Edward. "So tell me—do you really believe in happily ever after?"

He slid his arm around my waist. "I do now."

About the Author

Kathleen Fox grew up on a South Dakota farm, where listening to family dinner-table conversations made her a story addict. She is the author of *Making the Best of Second Best* and the co-author with Rick Kahler, CFP, of *Conscious Finance*. In her blog at practicalprairie.com, she takes a wry look at life's misadventures but embellishes only when strictly necessary.